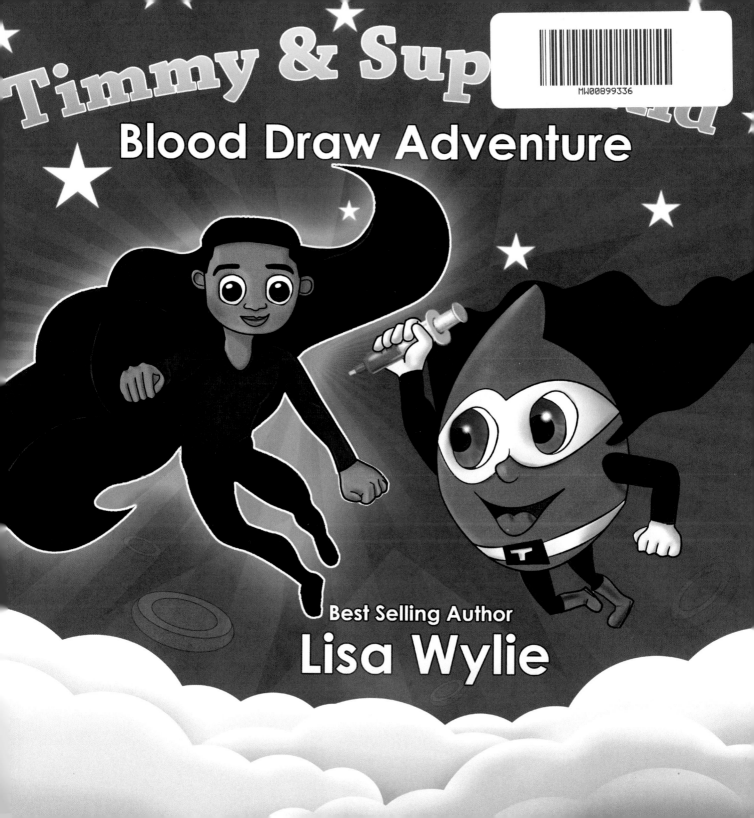

Title: Timmy Drop Blood Draw Adventures
Lab Team Assistants, LLC Production 2018

Author: Lisa Wylie
Illustrator: Lisa Wylie

Author Bio

Lisa Wylie has over twenty-three years of lab experience working in a variety of settings and specializes in working with all ages and special needs. She owns and operates Lab Team Assistants,LLC which is a mobile Phlebotomy Company that provides lab service in the clients home or office. Lisa has been teaching Phlebotomy classes for eleven years and also provides training to those looking to start their own Phlebotomy Businesses.

www.labteamassistants.com
www.labteamassistantstraining.com

Lab Team Assistants, LLC
Care Close To Home

"Dedication"

Memory of my mom Laverne Dickens

Thanks to my Grandma Mattie Andrews
who is always believing and supporting at all times.
Special thanks to my children
Timothy, Timesha, Teshawn, Arthur
for inspiration.
My siblings,family and friends
for believing and supporting me.
and to the lab staff everywhere.

"Woo-woo! Woo-woo!"
Timmy, the little blood drop
woke up with a hop and a splash.
The loud alarm and the flashing
lights only meant one thing.

A child needed help!
Timmy Blood Drop spun three
times on the air and took off. His
bright black cape flowed behind
him like Superman's cape.

He flew into the open window of a car and landed on a boy's lap.

"Who are you?" the boy whispered.

"I'm Timmy Blood Drop." Timmy whispered back.
"How do you like to be a superhero like me?"

The boy looked at Timmy with big eyes, "Really?! I can be a superhero?"
Timmy nodded, "and you will get to save the day!"
The boy jumped on his seat, "Yes, I want to be a superhero! Do I get to wear a cool superhero outfit?"

Timmy smiled, then hopped on the boy's shoulder
and whispered in his ear, "We are going on a secret mission.
You have to wear your regular clothes so you won't get discovered."

"What's the mission?" the boy asked excitedly.
Timmy took out a roll of paper and spread it out in front of the boy.
"Our mission for the day is to get blood drawn," Timmy explained.
"What's that? Will it hurt?" the boy asked.

"To get your blood drawn means that you have to go to a testing center and let a lab assistant take a little bit of your blood. It will feel like a little pinch, and it will be over very quickly," Timmy explained.

The boy looked away, "What if I'm scared?"

Timmy squeezed his hand, "It's alright to be scared, but I know that you are the bravest superhero of all and I'll be there with you all the way!"

The boy sighed, "Ok, I'll try to be brave."

There were pictures on the paper like a chart.

Timmy explained the steps of their secret mission by hopping from picture to picture.

There were pictures of driving to a large building, sitting in a room with many chairs,

then of a boy walking to a small room
and a lab assistant looking over his outstretched arm.

The boy thought,
this doesn't look too hard.
Looking at Timmy, he said,
"I'm ready to save the day!"

HOSPITAL

The car zoomed down the streets, and soon they parked in front of the large building on the first picture of the chart.

When they walked in, a smiling lady behind a desk with a small window said, "Good morning!"
"What's next?" the boy asked Timmy.

"Now we put your name on this list," Timmy said,
hopping to the counter where the smiling lady handed them a clipboard.

"I don't like waiting," said the boy.
Timmy smiled, "How about we do something fun?"
The boy smiled brightly, "Can we draw?"

HOSPITAL

HOSPITAL RECEPTION

DOCTOR

Timmy nodded, crossing down the steps they had done on their chart.
Then, he clapped his hands, and a notebook with blank sheets of paper
and crayons appeared in front of them.

Timmy and the boy drew a big picture of Timmy Blood Drop and Super Kid flying through the City in their superhero outfits.

A lab assistant called the boy's name,
and Timmy hopped into the boy's open hand.
"Remember, if you feel scared, just squeeze me as
hard as you can!"

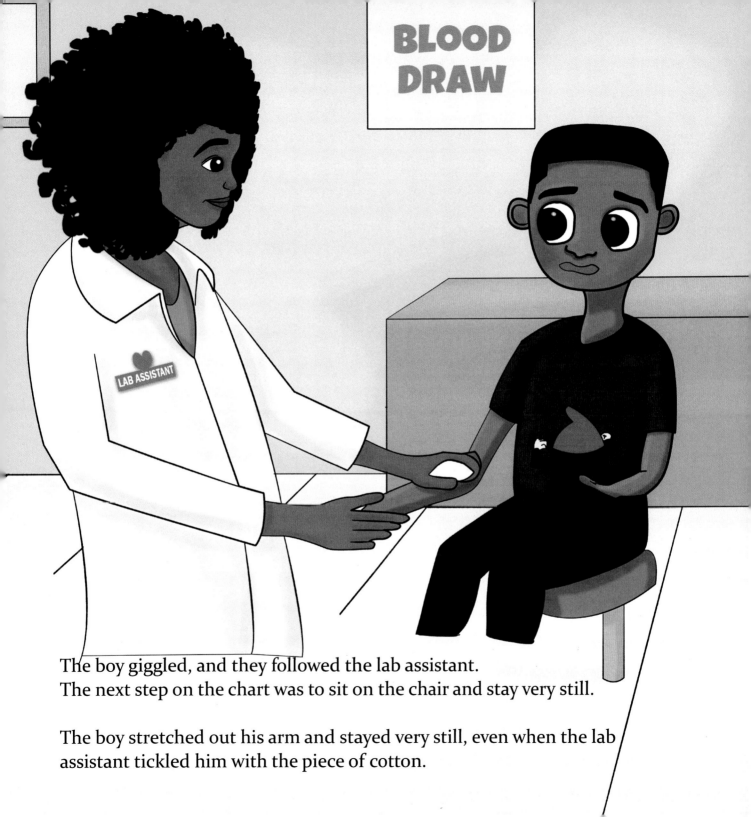

The boy giggled, and they followed the lab assistant.
The next step on the chart was to sit on the chair and stay very still.

The boy stretched out his arm and stayed very still, even when the lab
assistant tickled him with the piece of cotton.

"You are doing great!" Timmy said, sitting on the boy's open hand.

"Ready?" the lab assistant asked with a smile.

The boy nodded and took a deep breath.
His hand closed tightly around Timmy blood drop.
Timmy squeaked loudly, and the boy giggled.
He didn't even feel the little pinch of the needle on his arm.

"You are so brave!" Timmy squeaked.

The boy smiled, feeling proud.

But when he looked at the little bottles filling up with his blood, he frowned. "Isn't that a lot of blood?" he asked.

Timmy shook his head, "This is only a little bit of blood. Your body makes lots and lots of blood. By letting the lab assistant take this little, you are saving the day in a big way."

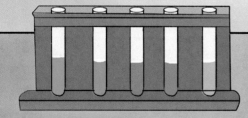

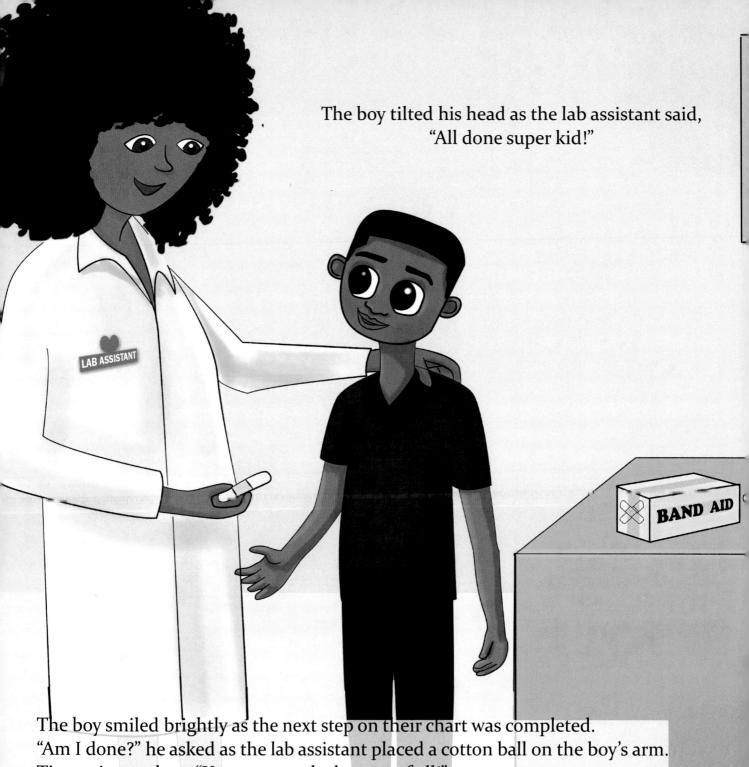

The boy tilted his head as the lab assistant said,
"All done super kid!"

BAND AID

The boy smiled brightly as the next step on their chart was completed.
"Am I done?" he asked as the lab assistant placed a cotton ball on the boy's arm.
Timmy jumped up, "Yes, you are, the bravest of all!"

Timmy explained, "Having your blood taken will save your body from mean germs that make you sick."

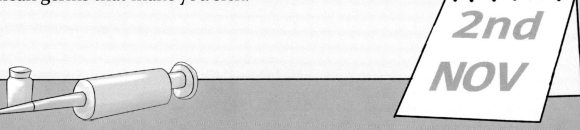

2nd NOV

The lab assistant smiled and held out two Band-Aids to the boy, "pick one."

The boy picked the one with happy faces and Timmy announced, "The day is safe!"

They flew out of the testing center giggling and laughing.
Getting blood drawn wasn't bad at all!

Timmy & Super Kid
Blood Draw Adventure

Timmy and Super-kid
are going to the hospital
to draw blood from super-kid.

Made in the USA
Monee, IL
21 July 2021

73210872R00019